Six Dinner Sid

For Richard

A catalogue record of this book is available from the British Library.

ISBN: 978 0 340 89411 8

Copyright © 1990 Inga Moore

The right of Inga Moore to be identified as the author of this Work has been asserted by her in accordance with the Copyright, Designs and Patents Act 1988.

First published in Great Britain in 1990 by
Simon & Schuster Young Books

This edition published in 2000
by Hodder Children's Books
a division of Hachette Children's Books
An Hachette Livre UK Company
338 Euston Road
London NW1 3BH

04

Printed in China

Six Dinner Sid

by
INGA MOORE

Hodder Children's Books

A division of Hachette Children's Books

Sid lived at number one, Aristotle Street.

He also lived at number two, number three,
number four, number five and number six.

Sid lived in six houses so that he could have
six dinners. Each night he would slip out
of number one, where he might have
had chicken, into number
two for fish…

on to number three for lamb,

mince at number four,

fish again at number five…

rounding off at number six
with beef and kidney stew.

Since no one talked to their neighbours
in Aristotle Street, no one knew what
Sid was up to. They each believed
the cat they fed was theirs,
and theirs alone.

But Sid had to work hard for his dinners. It wasn't easy being six people's pet. He had six different names to remember and six different ways to behave.

When he was being Scaramouche, Sid put on swanky airs.

As Bob he had a job.

He was naughty as Satan…

and silly as Sally.

As Sooty he smooched…

but as Schwartz he had to act rough and tough.

All this work sometimes wore Sid out. But he didn't care, as long as he had his six dinners. And, besides, he liked being...

scratched in six different places...

and sleeping in six different beds.

In fact, life in
Aristotle Street
was just about
perfect for Sid,
until…

one cold damp day, he caught a nasty cough.

The next thing he knew,
he was being taken to see the vet.
Poor Sid, he was taken not once…

not twice…

but six times!
He went with six different people,
in six different ways.

The vet said Sid's cough wasn't nearly as nasty as it sounded, but, to be on the safe side, he should have a spoonful of medicine.

Of course, Sid didn't have just one spoonful of medicine.

He had six!

Now, one black cat does look much like another, but nobody, not even a busy vet, could see the same cat six times without becoming suspicious. Sure enough, when he checked in his appointment book, the vet found six cats with a cough – all living in Aristotle Street!

So he rang the owners at once…

and, oh dear, Sid was found out!
When they discovered what he had been up to,
Sid's owners were furious. They said he had
no business eating so many dinners.

They said, in future, they would make sure
he had only one dinner a day.

But Sid was a six-dinner-a-day cat.
So he went to live at number one, Pythagoras Place.
He also went to live at numbers two, three, four,
five and six.

Unlike Aristotle Street, the people who lived in Pythagoras Place talked to their neighbours. So, right from the start, everyone knew about Sid's six dinners.

And, because everyone knew,
nobody minded.